The Please and Thank You Book

By Barbara Shook Hazen
Illustrated by Emilie Chollat

A GOLDEN BOOK · NEW YORK

Text copyright © 1974 by Random House, Inc. Illustrations copyright © 2009 by Emilie Chollat. All rights reserved.
Published in the United States by Golden Books, an imprint of Random House Children's Books, a division of
Random House, Inc., 1745 Broadway, New York, NY 10019. The material in this book originally appeared as part
of *Animal Manners*, published in 1974 in different form by Western Publishing Company, Inc. Golden Books,
A Golden Book, A Little Golden Book, the G colophon, and the distinctive gold spine are registered
trademarks of Random House, Inc.
www.goldenbooks.com
www.randomhouse.com/kids
Educators and librarians, for a variety of teaching tools, visit us at www.randomhouse.com/teachers
Library of Congress Control Number: 2008922396
ISBN: 978-0-375-84758-5
Printed in the United States of America
10 9 8 7
First Random House Edition 2009

Bears Always Share

Bears share their toys.
Bears share their honey.
Bears share a joke
They think is funny.

Whatever they do,
Whatever they wear,
They share it with
Another bear.

Watch Out for Wanda Warthog!

When Wanda Warthog comes over, beware!
She leaves a trail everywhere.
There's ink on the sofa, gum on the cat,
Modeling clay ground into the mat.

Her dirty fingerprints streak the wall.
She's broken her best friend's favorite doll.
Oops! There goes her dish of raspberry ice.
That's why poor Wanda is never asked twice.

Welcome,
Ricky Raccoon!

When Ricky Raccoon comes over to play,
He helps put all of the toys away.
He asks his friend what he'd like to do
And is always careful with scissors and glue.

He washes before he comes to the table
And helps his host whenever he's able.
That's why almost every day
Someone invites Ricky over to play.

Don't Be Grabby, Gorilla

Gorillas are rude.
They grab their food.
They never say,
"Please pass the peach."
They're so anxious,
They just reach.
They upset others
By all they do.
And sometimes . . . they upset
The table, too.

The Ox Always Knocks

The ox
Always knocks
Before
Opening a door.

Because
Someone behind it
Might be sleeping,
Or wrapping a present,
Or sad and weeping.

Then he always asks,
"May I come in?"
And everyone says,
"How thoughtful of him!"

Rabbits at the Table

The rabbit twins always taste
The food that's on the table.
They don't always eat it all,
But they eat as much as they're able.
Funny, or runny, or something new,
They try at least a bite or two.

Pull Yourself Together, Pamela Pig

Pamela Pig
Is simply a mess.
Her hair's uncombed.
There's ink on her dress.
Her hands are filthy,
And I have a hunch
That chocolate pudding
Was part of her lunch.
Doesn't she know
It isn't polite
To make others look
At such a sad sight?

Not So Wild, Cats!

Wildcats make their mother roar
The way they slam the kitchen door.
If they would close it quietly,
They'd see how pleased their mom would be.

Leopards Look Before They Leap

Leopards look before they leap.
They cross only with the light.
And when they cross
A crowded street,
They try to keep
To the right.

Elephants Remember

Thoughtful elephants
Always remember
To wipe their muddy feet.
They come inside
When their feet are dried.
They're really very neat.

Greta Goat, the Careless Kid

Greta Goat's a careless kid.
She loses everything.
Yesterday she lost her purse, and
Now she's lost her ring.
How it happens or where they are
Greta never knows.
If she's lucky, maybe she'll find them
Under that pile of clothes.

Terrible Tigers

Tiger cubs bicker
Night and day,
Day and night,
Whenever they play.
They bicker about
What they eat.
They bicker as they
Go to sleep.
Sister and brother
Scream at each other,
"You did it!"
"I *didn't*!"
"Yes, you did too!"
"No, I didn't!"
"You know it was you!"
They bicker and battle
So constantly,
They drive their poor mother
Straight up a tree.

"Play fair," says the hare,
"In all that you do.
Take only the turn
That's coming to you.

"Never cheat.
Never sneak.
When playing cards,
Never peek.

"Don't run before
The count of three.
And if you lose,
Lose gracefully.

"Hey! Now I see you
Laughing and grinning.
I guess you played fair
And ended up winning!"

Smile, Crocodile

How sad, how sad, Claude Crocodile.
He never greets anyone with a smile.
His mood is always gloomy and gray.
No wonder his friends go the opposite way.

Be Glad You're You!

The leopard is proud
Of her spotted coat,
The nightingale
Of his song.
The elephant's glad
She has a trunk.
The lion's glad
He's strong.

They all agree.
"I'm glad I'm me.
No one's more fun
Or nicer to be."